Amish Christmas Magic

By
Ruth Bawell

Table of Contents

Unsolicited Testimonials

By **Phyllis**

⭐⭐⭐⭐⭐ **Love Ruth!**

I love Ruth's books! Her mysteries are the best!

⭐⭐⭐⭐⭐ **Love This Author**

Ruth Bawell is very creative and a great writer! All her books have left me unable to stop reading till the ending! There were a few Amish fact mistakes, like unmarried man having a beard, but the plot was so good I overlooked that!

By **Steve M**

⭐⭐⭐⭐⭐ **I love romance stories** August 5, 2017
I love romance stories... well written with her usual twists to the story still enjoyed them very much Once I start I can't put it down.

By **Bones**

⭐⭐⭐⭐⭐ **Amish County Stories**
I love all the Amish County stories! Each one brings so much excitement! Ruth Bawell is also a wonderful writer!

By **Kindle Customer**

⭐⭐⭐⭐⭐ **Good clean writing.**
The Amish stories of Ruth Bawell are authentic, faith-filled writings. They are short, more the length of novellas or longer short stories. Always clean, always uplifting.

THE SUMMER BEFORE

There was a knock on the door that early Saturday morning. The late May breeze blew through the Fisher house with delight, and Abigail looked to her older sister Trina and her mother, who exchanged a knowing glance with each other. Her father stood up and walked over to the door, opening it. Abigail heard the familiar voice of Aaron Zook.

Aaron Zook, she thought dreamily. Her childhood schoolmate turned best friend. Of her nineteen years of life, she couldn't remember a time when he wasn't her best friend. And when he walked into the living room with his hat in his hands, she beamed. His eyes glowed with pride and love, and her heart soared. Today was finally the day Aaron Zook would ask to court her.

"Mrs. Fisher, Miss Abigail," he greeted with a nod to each of them. Abigail was quickly confused. *Why would he address her first?* He turned to her older sister Trina, a huge smile on his face. Her sister positively glowed with the attention, her eyes bright with excitement. "Miss Trina, would you like to accompany me to breakfast this morning?"

And Abigail's heart shattered.

She watched, faking a smile as her sister accepted the invitation. Her mother clapped, and Aaron shook hands with her father. She bit back tears, wanting nothing more than to go to her small room in the attic that she loved so much and stitch away the day. Maybe she could finish her quilt finally, and probably start and finish a second one as well. Lord knew she was going to need the spend the whole day praying and crying, away from the company of others.

As the front door shut, it felt as if Aaron had shut the door on their friendship as well. Abigail politely dismissed herself, claiming to need to wash for breakfast with her parents. She went to the small sink on the main floor, splashing her face and washing her hands from the spigot.

She felt the tears fall down her cheeks. Abigail realized she must have spent a considerable time at the sink, as her mother came to check on her. Upon seeing her crying, Dorothy Fisher wrapped Abigail in a hug. And Abigail just wept harder.

"Don't worry, dear," her mother soothed. "You haven't lost either one of them."

I'm grieving for myself, she thought with some distaste. She didn't want to be jealous of Trina, but she couldn't stop the feeling or its physical manifestations. But as she was cradled into the embrace, she couldn't bear to correct her mother's thinking. It was too shameful to even admit such a thing.

***

It had been three months since Aaron and Trina had started courting. A long three months. It felt like the summer would never end, that Trina would never start her work teaching at the schoolhouse and Aaron would be busy on the farm. In fact, it seemed as if the couple had so much extra time on their hands that they were going out on dates daily.

That day, Abigail had been so graciously invited to accompany them on their afternoon stroll through the town. Despite her insistence that she wanted to continue her work on her quilt that Mrs. Schwartz had paid her to make for their upcoming granddaughter, Trina and Aaron all but forced her to stop and dragged her along with them.

So there she was, walking with them that August afternoon, listening to the couple talk and babble about whatever futures they saw with each other—none of which it seemed included Abigail. She couldn't help but think that this whole outing had just taken away time from her quilting.

"I'm really glad you joined us," Trina smiled, looking across Aaron to where Abigail was on his other side. "I've been missing time with my sister."

"And I have missed my best friend," Aaron added. "I'm glad we could all have this time together."

Well, if only you could not hang out with each other all the time, then maybe you wouldn't be missing me, Abigail thought bitterly. After internally expressing her anger, she sent an apology to God for acting so childish and unsupportive. But she couldn't help but feel… angry. Taking a deep breath, she forced the anger down to the ground, leaving it behind as she walked.

"Thanks for inviting me," was all Abigail said instead, her plastered-on smile that she had mastered rather fast appearing once again. "It is a really beautiful day."

"Anytime. You're like a sister to me," he smiled, nudging her shoulder politely. "And I thought, well… Trina and I get along so well, and you and I are best friends. It seemed natural!"

Abigail agreed, plastering on her smile even more thickly. Aaron's hand didn't leave Trina's as they walked along the path. Her sister laughed at something Aaron had said, a joke that Abigail had probably heard a hundred times herself. She felt as if she was slipping away from both of them— fitting in neither as Trina's sister nor as Aaron's friend.

She looked out past the county borders, in the direction of Lancaster county. Abigail wanted to break out into a run, not stopping until she got to Uncle Wayne's house in Lancaster. She wanted a fresh start, away from Trina and Aaron. Watching them together over the summer hurt more than Abigail cared to admit. God was working silently in her life and in her prayers, but she still felt a little lost.

"Abigail?" Her sister's voice drifted to her ears. Abigail shook her head, coming back to the present moment. "Is everything alright?"

"Oh, it's nothing," she lied. "Just thinking about a quilt patch like that sky over there."

"Always stuck in your head with the quilting," Aaron joked kindly, but for some reason, it stung. "Baking is where it's at."

Trina laughed, and Abigail smiled politely. She was the only quilter of the

Fisher women. And it was something she enjoyed doing. It was not that her mother and sister were unkind to her about it, but they were so connected because they both liked to bake. Whereas unless she was canning and making jams, Abigail was almost helpless in the kitchen.

I want to go to Lancaster, she thought, her eyes returning to the direction of the neighboring county. With the money from Mrs. Schwartz, it could be possible to ask for a room at Uncle Wayne's, at least for the first two months. And it would also cover her travel there if her parents or the Lambrights couldn't transport her. But it was all a silly wish.

Abigail decided to turn that wish into a prayer, asking God to show her a way forward at least. Suddenly there was a strong breeze from behind them. It was so strong Abigail's prayer cap almost flew off her head, and she held it down with both hands as her feet slid along the gravel towards Lancaster. But she couldn't help but smile, happy tears brimming in her eyes as she looked to the distance.

God had answered.

CHAPTER ONE

<u>THE FALL</u>

It was a normal day in the woodshop with Mr. Lambright. There was carving to be done and finished for the church, and Caleb would finally get a chance to start on the new table he had designed. He yawned, looking at the sun out the window, approaching the midpoint in the sky. Twenty years of being alive, and he never got used to seeing the sun in all of God's glory.

Caleb Graber had been up since the sun started to peek above the horizon, helping his brother, Sawyer, with the harvest season fast approaching. It was late August, and even though Sawyer was taking over the Graber farm with his wife, Bridget, next year, Caleb still felt connected to the land. To the farm. So it was all hands on deck.

That was his whole life, as a matter of fact.

Caleb was never in one place too long, and he liked it that way—it kept him busy. Besides, the Father Above had granted him ample strength and faculty to labor, so it seemed an afront to waste it away. It may not have pleased everyone he ever met, but it pleased him and God, so that was all that Caleb cared about.

Except, it did get lonely.

Shaking his head of the negative thoughts, he went on out to the main store area of the woodshop, ready for lunch. Apparently, Mrs. Lambright had promised it, and she always made the best lunches, consisting of fresh, simple sandwiches and lemonade. They were delicious, and Caleb wouldn't trade them for the world.

But instead of Mrs. Lambright or Patience, their daughter, walking into the shop, it was someone new. She carried the cooler from the Lambright house. She had bright blue eyes that were as clear as the lakes and ginger-colored hair. She smiled, the smattering of freckles across her face moving with her grin. She was shorter than him, though not by much, and quite slender.

The shop bell dinged, breaking Caleb out of his trance. There was Mrs. Eleanor Lambright and Patience, as he originally expected. They smiled warmly at him. The women walked up to the counter.

"Good afternoon, Caleb," Mrs. Lambright greeted. "Hungry as ever I see."

"Always when it comes to your sandwiches and lemonade, Mrs. Lambright," he smiled. "I could eat them every day."

"But then they wouldn't be special," Mrs. Lambright smiled.

Mr. Wayne Lambright appeared from his private office, his glasses perched on his nose. He smiled as he took in the women standing at the door. Caleb really liked his boss—Mr. Lambright had taught him a lot about carpentry, and they were well-respected in the community. If anyone wanted anything made, they came to him, which meant that there was never a lack of work to be done.

Mr. Lambright smiled and went to give his wife and daughter a hug, along with the newcomer. Lancaster might have been a big community, but Caleb was sure he would have recognized the girl. Not to mention, she was breathtakingly beautiful, her eyes drawing him in.

"Caleb, have you been introduced to my niece?" Mr. Lambright asked, motioning to the other girl.

He shook his head, "I haven't had the pleasure yet, sir. Caleb Graber, miss."

"Abigail Fisher," she replied, her voice delicate and soft. "It's nice to meet you."

Abigail, he thought in his head dreamily. It suited her, and he smiled at the sound of her voice. She was beautiful, and simply so. He took the cooler laden with their lunches from her gratefully, a seeming connection passing between them in the air.

"She just moved in with us a few days ago and will be helping Eleanor around the house, and I'm sure quilting away," Mr.

Lambright explained. "She's a mighty fine quilter."

"Uncle Wayne, you are too kind." Abigail blushed.

"My mother quilts." Caleb smiled kindly at her, still feeling affected from her touch. He wasn't one to make small talk and usually kept to himself. "I'm sure you'll be meeting her at Church on Sunday. She loves to have quilting circles."

"That sounds like a grand time," Abigail smiled.

"You know, Caleb, your mother is simply going to have to let us invite *her* for once," Mrs. Lambright laughed.

They all joined in, even Abigail. Her laugh sounded like little bells, and Caleb couldn't help but sneak another glance in her direction. Her eyes were already on him, and she looked away quickly, a pink color coming to her cheeks. Maybe she felt a spark too…

But when would he ever have the time? And he couldn't—recover from another heartbreak. After Collette had broken their courtship because he worked too much, Caleb had dedicated himself even more to both the farm and the shop. It was the only relief he could find from the pain.

He watched as the Lambrights and Abigail left the shop. There was something about Abigail that stuck with him long after she had left. It followed him throughout the day and when he had gone home for the evening chores. If it was meant to be, God would bring them together. He had faith in that.

But until then, he'd keep working.

CHAPTER TWO

They walked out of the carpentry store, her mind still whirring. Caleb Graber was one of the most handsome men she had ever met. With green eyes that looked like soft meadows and ruddy brown hair, he was objectively good-looking. Not to mention, *tall*. But his smile, the smooth timbre of his voice, that is what drew Abigail in.

"I've never heard Caleb Graber talk that much in one conversation," Aunt Eleanor laughed.

"It's because Abigail was there," her cousin Patience teased, nudging her shoulder. "You can't tell me you didn't see him looking at you!"

Abigail simply laughed—she hadn't come here to fall in love. In fact, she was trying to do the exact opposite. Her time in Lancaster, though somewhat short, had already felt like the right decision. She had been here for three days and was already welcomed into the folds of the community and the household of Uncle Wayne, Aunt Eleanor, and Patience.

And funnily enough, she hadn't even thought about Aaron Zook or Trina once.

They got in the buggy and headed to the Lambright house. Uncle Wayne had graciously taken her in without asking a cent, her work around the house help enough. And there was a lot to do helping Aunt Eleanor with the sewing she took in, so she was grateful to always have something to do. She was even awarded her own room, and she felt very comfortable. Even though only sixteen, Patience already felt more like a sister to her than Trina had sometimes felt.

And not to mention the quilting she could do.

Aunt Eleanor and Patience loved to quilt as much as she did. They had a wondrous supply of fabrics, and they had even taken her to Spector's to go pick out some that she liked. Abigail had never gone shopping for fabric before. Her parents either mail-ordered it, or it was gifted to her. She could spend a whole day just *looking* at the bolts on the shelf.

"Abigail?" her aunt's voice called out to her. She refocused her attention back to the conversation, realizing that they had arrived back home. "Is everything alright?"

"Oh, I was just thinking about the fabric at Spector's," she smiled.

"I know, right?!" Patience jumped giddily. "They have so much! I could spend days in there. But if you think that's impressive, wait until Mrs. Graber holds a quilting circle!"

"Does she host them often?" Abigail couldn't help but ask.

Aunt Eleanor laughed. "Once a month out on the Graber farm. They have a large basement and people come from all over, even some from other counties. We quilt, trade fabric and tricks, and talk about the Father. It's very… renewing."

"Agreed." Patience nodded.

Abigail was so excited, and she hoped that Mrs. Graber would invite her along. She had never been to a community-wide quilting circle before. The mere thought of sitting in a chair, quilting away with other people like her, and praising God had her excited. She couldn't think of a better way to spend an evening.

***

For the first month in Lancaster, Abigail stayed busy. And apparently, so did Caleb Graber. She barely saw him at all, even when she volunteered to take lunch to the shop. He was there physically, but she could see his mind was elsewhere. She had to smile one time at his distant stare, wondering if she looked the same way when she dreamt about her quilts.

But from what Aunt Eleanor told her, he helped on the family farm, with the busy harvest season coming up. She had noticed that even Uncle Wayne was gone most of the day at the shop with all the special Christmas gifts that had been ordered from him, many from the English townspeople nearby. So, of course, Caleb was busy.

She couldn't help but be in awe at his dedication. Although her heart sank at the seemingly dying connection between them, she knew that if it was meant to be, God would see to it that it would happen. Until then, he had to continue with his obligations, and she respected that.

Besides, she had her own matters to attend to as well. With a third seamstress available, Aunt Eleanor could bring more sewing in from the community and even make some extra money with the quick turnaround. And she even spent time baking! Her aunt and cousin were incredibly patient with Abigail in the kitchen, teaching her basic cookie recipes and breads.

One afternoon, she sat on one of the rockers, gently swaying as she tried a new stitch with Patience. It was hard to waste even the smallest scrap of fabric, but both girls wanted to try the new stitch that Aunt Eleanor had just mastered. Not to mention, it looked like little flowers, and Abigail's mind ran with all the ideas for spring quilts she could make.

"Are you getting it down?" Patience asked.

Abigail shook her head a little side to side. "So-So."

"Abigail, you have a letter," her aunt called.

Abigail set down her quilt and walked over to where Aunt Eleanor was holding a plain brown envelope. She tore it open, seeing the address from her family's house.

She had written them at least once a week, updating them per her father's kind request. As she pulled out the letter, she noticed her father's handwriting first.

He wished her well and was glad that things were going so well in Lancaster. He had enclosed scripture verses from Bishop Emmanuel that she might like and had even mailed her a little money to spend on fabric at Spector's. She smiled—she missed her family a lot, but she felt at peace in Lancaster.

Her mother's handwriting appeared next, with a handwritten recipe for apple pie. Apparently, her mother had tweaked it enough so that it was just a bit sweeter like Abigail always liked, and now she could try with Aunt Eleanor and Patience.

As she unfolded the letter to read the recipe, a smaller paper floated to the ground. Confused, Abigail bent down and picked it up. She flipped it over to see her sister's and Aaron's handwriting compiled on the card. She read it through twice, almost not believing her eyes.

A wedding announcement.

CHAPTER THREE

The rest of the day that Thursday, she felt…
glum. She was happy for her sister and
Aaron, but some small part of her was still a
little jealous. Not as hurt as she once was
that Aaron had courted Trina and not her,
but she saw how happy the two were with
each other. Despite herself, she couldn't
help but want that a little too.

*There is surely a hope for you, and
your hope will not be cut off*, Abigail recited
silently. Proverbs 23:18—it had always been
one of her favorite verses. But it wasn't as
comforting as she wanted it to be. And while
she had prayed and talked with God, there
was still something nagging her about the
whole courtship between Aaron and Trina.

She wanted to talk to someone who knew what she was dealing with. But she didn't know who, and she didn't want to ask. Somewhere deep in her heart, she still felt shame for all her feelings. Even though she hadn't thought of Aaron since she had moved to Lancaster, it still seemed to sting.

Abigail sat on the floor next to Patience, carefully planning the look of the Northern Star for her Christmas quilt. It had come to her last night in a dream, and she couldn't wait to bring it to life with her family in their own private quilting circle that night.

"Abigail, is everything alright?" Aunt Eleanor asked, a kind smile on her face. "You seem a little quiet after reading the letter from your parents. Did something happen?"

Abigail shook her head, the tears threatening to spill out. She bit her lip, trying to take a deep breath and answer her aunt. But then Patience's arms came around her shoulder in a hug, and she couldn't hold it back anymore. She broke down in tears.

"Are you homesick?" her cousin asked, gently rubbing her back. "Or did something happen?"

"Trina and Aaron are getting married," Abigail managed, but it sounded like childish blubber even to her own ears.

"Oh sweetheart," Aunt Eleanor called, getting up from the rocker and joining them carefully on the floor, not disturbing even the smallest of threads. "What about it?"

At her aunt's kind voice, the words just fell out. Abigail confessed everything, her head hung in shame. She couldn't stop crying, either. She just wanted to be *over it* and happy for the couple, but her hurt still ran so deep, it seemed. She told her aunt and cousin the reason she asked to move, about her and Aaron's friendship. Everything, including her guilt and shame that she bared for being so angry and jealous.

At the end of her confession, she felt lighter for at least having spoken about it. But that didn't help the uneasy feelings she held. She looked to her aunt, who broke out into a smile and threw her head back… and laughed.

"Oh Abigail, you are such a tender heart," she cried with laughter. She hugged her niece tighter, "Honey, you aren't the only one who has ever felt jealous."

"Really?" Abigail asked, swatting at the tears.

"Oh goodness no," Eleanor laughed. "I felt the same way when I was just a little older than yourself. My cousin was being courted by the guy I liked, and he and I were actually schoolmates too. And I was so angry for a long time, and jealous too."

"How did you deal with it?" Abigail asked.

"Well, I didn't. But I managed. And funny enough, they ended up breaking the courtship off." She smiled. "About a month after they parted ways, he actually came to my house to ask me to lunch."

"Did you go?" the girls chorused with curiosity.

"Nope," Aunt Eleanor said with a smile. "You see, there was a visitor to my community, learning carpentry, and he had asked me to go to lunch with him the day before. And I was much more smitten with him than I ever was with Jeremiah. So I had to turn him down, and I don't regret it a single day, because I got to marry that man and have a beautiful family."

"That's how you met Pa?" Patience asked with a bright smile. "Wow, lucky timing."

"It always is when God's in charge," Aunt Eleanor smiled. She turned to Abigail, squeezing her in a big hug. "It happens, my dear. God will not punish you for it, for you have not acted wrongly. Your heart is simply feeling things that are natural and part of the process of love."

Abigail felt comforted by the advice, knowing that there was someone she knew that had gone through it. And it seemed as if her aunt's story was the final push she needed to move forward. The three women fell into a hug of healing laughter, and Abigail sent a prayer to God, thanking him for blessing her with such an amazing family and support.

"Let's make apple pie tomorrow," Abigail smiled.

CHAPTER FOUR

It was mid-October before he ran into Abigail Fisher again—this time, almost literally. His mother was hosting her quilting circle that Wednesday night, and he almost collided with Abigail on his way up from the basement as he moved chairs down the stairs for the gathering. He caught her arms to keep her from falling and managed to catch the bag around her shoulder as well. Her small hands clutched his forearms tightly.

"So sorry, Miss Abigail," he apologized, holding on to her carefully.

"The fault is all mine," she smiled sweetly. "I'm afraid I was lost in thought."

As they righted themselves, he noticed a small corner of a quilt peeking out over the corner of the bag. It was blue, with swirls of white thread stitched in, and he could just barely see the white and yellow of the Christmas Star. It was some of the most beautiful quilting he had ever seen, and that was just a corner.

"Is that your quilt?" he asked curiously. She nodded, a blush appearing on her cheeks. "It is very beautiful. You have quite the skill. And the craft is impeccable. I can see why Mr. Lambright speaks so highly of your talent."

"Oh, thank you," she replied humbly. "God has gifted me, truly."

"Indeed He has," Caleb smiled down at her. He tipped his hat down to her, stepping out of the way of the stairs. "Have a good quilting evening, Miss Abigail."

***

She walked down the stairs to the Graber basement. Aunt Eleanor and Patience followed shortly thereafter. Abigail felt light as a feather. The compliment from Caleb Graber had set her whole being into a state of pure joy. Mrs. Greta Graber greeted her warmly with Aunt Eleanor and Patience, leading each of them to a rocker or pillow or chair.

You have quite the skill, Caleb had said.

She pulled her quilt out of her bag but was suddenly embarrassed. What if he was just being kind to her because he had to? What if it wasn't the compliment her heart thought it was? Doubt crept into her mind, and Abigail looked at the patch of the night sky.

The seams were terrible—the stitches didn't line up perfectly. She couldn't find any more of the same yellow fabric for the star, so she'd had to substitute white, which to her eyes did not quite look right. And not to mention, she had never quilted people into her quilts, and this vision required at least six of them.

"Oh goodness my," Mrs. Graber explained. Abigail turned to see the host's eyes wide with horror, focused on the patchwork of the sky. Abigail bent her head in shame. "Abigail, you have a gift!"

What? Abigail turned her head up to meet the older woman's kind smile. It was genuine. Something… sweet. She had meant the compliment, and Abigail thanked her host humbly. Soon she was getting a lot of oohs and aahs from the gathered crowd.

Aunt Eleanor smiled, simply bringing up her own patchwork and starting to quilt, beginning to rock in the chair.

Patience hugged Abigail around the shoulders and whispered in her ear, "You count yourself out too quickly. God has given you this amazing vision because He knows you have the talent to bring it to life."

"Thank you," Abigail whispered. "Sometimes my mind plays tricks on me."

"You are safe here," she smiled. "Besides, I never met a Graber who ever gave a compliment and didn't mean it."

The craft is impeccable, Caleb's voice rang through her head. She smiled at her cousin and believed her. Caleb had meant what he told her, and that was a lot coming from a craftsman like himself. She had seen the table he was working on in the shop—he had an eye for detail. And it made her smile to know that he thought so highly of her work.

Her heart was treading into some familiar territory, and she wasn't sure how she felt about that.

CHAPTER FIVE

That Sunday, after church, she continued the last stitches of her Christmas quilt. It had been odd when Aunt Eleanor and Patience had picked up their quilting the first Sunday she was in Lancaster. Her mother viewed it as work, and so, therefore, Abigail had avoided quilting on Sundays.

But for Aunt Eleanor and Patience, as long as they were not getting paid for the time spent, they quilted. They also had a rule that any quilts that they worked on Sundays were not to be sold at markets either. They were to be used for gifts or personal use only, and with the holidays coming up, there were plenty of gifts to go around. So that added yet another day for Abigail to quilt, and she worked on her Christmas quilt.

There was a knock at the door, and Uncle Wayne and Aunt Eleanor looked at each other quizzically. They weren't expecting visitors, and it was late in the afternoon. Uncle Wayne stood and made his way to the door. The women paused their quilting and waited. Soon, there was the merry voice of Bishop Samuel.

"Good afternoon, Lambrights and Fishers," he cheered, walking into the house. He saw the women working, a smile on his face. "Ah, the lovely trio of quilters."

"Indeed they are," Uncle Wayne said next to him. "God has truly blessed me with such a talented family. What brings you here on this blessed day?"

"I actually have a question for Miss Abigail," he said, turning to her kindly. "If she is receiving company, that is?"

Bishop Samuel was tall and had kind brown eyes and thin glasses. It seemed that every time she saw him, he was smiling. It was infectious. She smiled back and set down her thread and needle.

"I am," she answered. "What can I help you with?"

"Well, I have heard many people tell me about this Christmas quilt of yours," he started. "And so I was wondering if I could see it and if it was possibly for sale? It would be a great addition to the Christmas program this year. If not, no worries, dear."

She looked down at the backing she had almost finished and then to Aunt Eleanor. Her eyes met Patience's, and her cousin nodded with encouragement. *You count yourself out too quickly.* Abigail turned back to Bishop Samuel.

"It is only halfway done, but the scenery is complete," she answered.

She stood up and flipped over the quilt to show the nativity scene she had managed to make, just like her vision. The quilting circle at the Graber house had helped her a lot with the figures. Bishop Samuel's eyes went wide with admiration.

"Does it have a story?" he whispered softly. "And how much is it?"

"God gave me a vision," she answered. "It came to me in a dream, so I just had to quilt it. And I am terribly sorry, Bishop Samuel, but it's not for sale."

"Incredible talent," he hummed, his eyes downturned softly. "But I understand, Miss Abigail."

"However, I would like to gift it to the church once it's finished," she amended quickly. "I don't want the Father to think I have made His vision a piece of work, especially on a blessed day like today. You can have it, but I don't want any money for it."

"So very wise," he smiled at her and then turned to Aunt Eleanor. "I see you have taught her your rule."

Aunt Eleanor laughed, "Of course, Bishop Samuel."

"Let us pray," he cheered. The women put down their sewing, and the group joined hands. Abigail bowed her head and closed her eyes, and soon Bishop Samuel began the prayer:

"The Father Almighty has looked down on this family with love and grace here today. As stated in 1 Peter, 4:10, 'As each has received a gift, use it to serve one another, as good stewards of God's varied grace.' And He has blessed each of you with an incredible gift. Whether it be creation, leadership, or compassion, each of you has something amazing. Instead of being selfish and proud, you have gone forth and given of yourselves without expectation of return. And God sees that. May He bless you and the work that you do. Amen."

"Amen," they all chorused.

They raised their heads and opened their eyes. Abigail treasured this moment—she finally knew what it felt like to be so accepted in a community. Though, not that her home or her own family had made an outcast of her. But there was something altogether different about being in a place where your talent and work were celebrated.

"Thank you, Bishop Samuel," Uncle Wayne stated. "We are incredibly grateful for your leadership and commitment. Father's blessings to you and your work as we look towards a merry Christmas."

Bishop Samuel nodded with a large smile, "Thank you, Wayne. And thank you, Abigail. The Father has blessed this house and this community."

CHAPTER SIX

It had been almost a month since the quilting circle at the Graber farm. Caleb had seen Abigail here and there as the women brought them lunch, but he had not seen much of her. However, on that Sunday morning, there was a beautiful quilt hanging up in the church to bring in the holiday spirit. And he recognized the quilt.

It was Abigail's.

The quilt was stunning now that it was completed. The corner he had seen had paled in comparison to the finished product. It was wonderfully crafted, with love and honor for the Father in every stitch. Not to mention, it was the complete nativity scene in Bethlehem. It had taken her some time to complete it. He was impressed, and his mother had told him that she had never quilted people before.

Even so, seeing it made a rock sink in his stomach.

Bishop Samuel must have pursued her for it, given Caleb's earnest request that he do so a few weeks before. Still, he hadn't expected it to be displayed so proudly. The Lambrights must think of him as some sort of maniac, going around and doing nice things for Abigail without courting her.

That Monday morning, Caleb was fraught with nerves. Mr. Lambright walked into the shop, and he almost dropped the tools he was holding. His hands shook. Caleb turned to greet his boss, trying to look casual. But even he could see how much his body moved with nervousness.

"Good morning, Caleb," Mr. Lambright smiled. "Did you have a good weekend?"

"I did," he replied. "I was grateful the Father gave me some time to rest yesterday. And how was your weekend?"

"It was quite good," Mr. Lambright answered. "Bishop Samuel stopped by the house Saturday to pick up Abigail's finished quilt. I thought that it went well with the decorations. And the sermon at church was just lovely. What about you?"

Did he know? Caleb thought with panic. Had he overstepped his boundaries? Of course, he was just trying to be nice. He studied Mr. Lambright's face, trying to gauge the emotion he was feeling. He was smiling, but it didn't touch his eyes like it usually did.

"Is everything alright, Caleb?" Mr. Lambright asked, and Caleb realized he hadn't answered. "You look pale."

"I told Bishop Samuel!" he blurted.

Mr. Lambright looked at him, confused. "Told Bishop Samuel about what, Caleb?"

"Miss Abigail's quilt," he confessed. "I ran into her on accident when she was at the farm the other week for the quilting circle, and I saw the quilt. And my mother also commented on it. So I told him on Sunday after church that he should look at it. I'm so sorry, Mr. Lambright."

He dared a glance at his employer. But there was no anger—in fact, Mr. Lambright was smiling—all the way to his eyes. He just chuckled, walking over to Caleb with outstretched arms. He wrapped the younger man in a hug, laughing away.

"Oh my boy," he laughed. "Is that what has you so shaky?"

"I didn't mean to overstep my place, sir," he stammered. "But I thought that maybe Bishop Samuel would appreciate the work."

"Caleb, it's alright," Mr. Lambright soothed. "No one is mad. In fact, we were all very happy. Abigail gifted it to the church after she finished it shortly after he had visited. You didn't do anything wrong."

"It's immaculate," Caleb sighed with relief. "And I wanted her to get recognition for it, like you do for me here."

"She appreciated it," Mr. Lambright smiled. "Although, why aren't you telling Abigail these things?"

"I'm not sure it's the right time," he admitted. "The harvest is almost done, and I am still working on that table for the market next week."

Mr. Lambright smiled kindly at him, "Speaking of that, I have a question for you."

So the two men spent the morning talking about Caleb's future with the shop. In a few years, Mr. Lambright wanted to settle down and retire. Maybe he would spend time volunteering at the church and making things to his heart's content. But first, he wanted to see Patience married and settled before he committed to retirement, so the timeline was flexible.

So, it seemed that was more than enough time for Caleb to learn how to run the store and do the taxes. He could save enough money to buy the shop from Mr. Lambright, and even hire a new person to train if he had enough. With the shop doing so well this season, Caleb could put away a large chunk of his earnings to making that a reality.

When Mrs. Lambright, Patience, and Abigail all stopped by for lunch, which they stayed and ate themselves as well, Caleb was positively beaming. In a few short years, he was going to have something that he could call his own. Looking at Abigail, he wondered if maybe it could work out in the long run, with him owning a business and all.

But right now, he just needed a little more time.

CHAPTER SEVEN

That Saturday at the market was bitterly cold, but she was too excited to care. It was the last market of the season, given the weather trend and the cold beginnings of winter already upon them. She watched as Caleb and Uncle Wayne unloaded the table that Caleb had worked so hard on for so long. *Father Above, let him be rewarded*, she prayed.

Together, they set up a table of their quilts and little trinkets, Patience unveiling some new cards she had made for the holidays. Soon, there was a familiar warmth around her, and she saw Mrs. Graber and Bridget Graber walking up with the help of Caleb and another man she knew to be Sawyer, the elder of the brothers.

They were carrying boxes of what was revealed to be jars. There was elegant script on each of the labels, a variety of jams and jellies and preserves spread on the table. Abigail looked in awe, wondering how one family could can so much food! Not to mention decorating the lids with ribbons and bows too!

"I've always wanted to learn how to can," Patience said softly, watching them unpack the boxes. "It looks like it would be so much fun."

"It is," Abigail and Mrs. Graber chorused together.

The two women looked at each other and began to laugh. Soon, they were talking about canning and how they could produce so much. Abigail listened in awe at the process of Bridget and Greta Graber at their kitchen table after harvest season. Even Aunt Eleanor and Patience were sharing the enthusiasm after a while.

"You should come by our house one afternoon," Aunt Eleanor smiled. "It would be so much fun to learn how to do all of that! Besides, I have all the supplies ready to go. I haven't had time to can the berries Caleb gave us from the harvest."

"We could make a pie too!" Patience added. "I have been craving some Graber cherry pie lately."

"And we could quilt afterwards!" Bridget clapped excitedly.

"Oh, that all sounds delightful," Mrs. Graber joined in. "What day works best, Eleanor?"

So the women made a plan to visit the following Tuesday night. Abigail could hardly wait, especially with how much money she had saved up from the sale of her quilts at the market recently, plus the small amounts her father sent with every letter. She just knew their weekly shopping trip to Spector's was going to bring in a lot of little trims for the cans and the quilts.

Everything just seemed to be coming together so well.

***

Caleb overheard Abigail and Mrs. Lambright talking with his mother and sister-in-law about canning that weekend at the market. He smiled at how the two families were so close, and he wished that he had time to court Abigail properly. Maybe after the winter, he could. But with the shop working around the clock to finish orders, it was too much for him to ask of Abigail.

Just a little more time.

He could take a day off, but it seemed rude to ask Mr. Lambright for his permission and for a day off all at once. Not to mention, how awkward it would be if he denied Caleb on either account. So far, he had held firm that he would wait for God to show him the right time, but he was torn in thinking that he had maybe worked away the extra time the Father had given him.

A customer came up to him. She was an English woman, and her eyes went to his beautiful, handcrafted table. He greeted her kindly, and she smiled warmly at him. They got to talking about all of the things he had created within the table, even configuring a way to have the stow-away table leaf in there.

"It is very beautiful," she complimented. "And it's unstained?"

"Yes, ma'am," he smiled. "That way, you can match it to your current furniture."

"That is exactly what I'm looking for," she smiled. "My husband's daughter is getting married next weekend, and we wanted to gift them a dining table. But their house is being remodeled, and they haven't decided on a color scheme yet for the cabinets."

Caleb laughed at the story along with the woman, and by the time they had recovered, she had offered to buy it—at twice the listed cost. Caleb told her as much, but she insisted she would pay nothing less than what she offered. It was Christmas, after all.

"Besides, maybe this can buy back some time," she smiled, handing him the considerable sum of money. "Merry Christmas, Caleb."

His jaw almost dropped to the ground—he hadn't told her his name.

CHAPTER EIGHT

That next Tuesday night was abuzz with activity in the Lambright house. The Graber women had joined them for canning and quilting long before Uncle Wayne came home from the shop. They were so easy to get along with, and they kept great company.

And the Grabers sure knew a lot about canning.

Abigail watched and mentally took notes for her sister and mother. It was something amazing to watch how seamlessly Bridget and Mrs. Graber worked together when they got in the swing of the rhythm.

After they had finished all they could together, Aunt Eleanor and Patience watching them eagerly, they made a fresh pie. Having five women in the kitchen proved to be one of the best experiences Abigail had ever been a part of. There was no shortage of laughter to be heard in such a company.

Once the pie was done, they sat down to quilt. Abigail never could get enough of her craft. It was too exciting and too much fun, especially with other people. Watching Mrs. Graber as she started a new quilt was an art form within itself. Bridget showed her the sketch of the quilt she was going to make over the winter and revealed that she was expecting a baby.

"We should make a patchwork quilt," her cousin suggested. "And each of us could make the patches and sew it together."

"That's a great idea, Patience!" Mrs. Graber complimented. "After the new year starts, we can do that at quilting circle!"

"Maybe even extend it to the community," Abigail asked. "Wouldn't that be lovely? Like a little square of each of us, all sewn together? Like God imagined on that day he made man."

"Greta, let us host a small circle here first for that," Aunt Eleanor insisted kindly. "You can keep your once-a-month circle, and we'll be there for that too, but let's keep our patchwork quilt to ourselves for a bit. That way, we can figure out all the snags without as many people."

"You know, I was just about to say something similar," Bridget laughed. "Besides, I've been dying to learn that little flower stitch from you, Mrs. Lambright.

Father knows I'll have enough time throughout the pregnancy to perfect it before the baby arrives."

***

Abigail wrote a second letter to her family that night, she was so happy. She told them some of the Graber secrets for canning in hopes that they could have similar success with their jams, and said she couldn't wait to see them again and tell them all about Lancaster in person.

Abigail explained who the Grabers were and hoped her family could meet them all one day. She told them about their idea to create a patchwork quilt, the five of them. She said that if it went well, they could do a larger community one too. Abigail also attached a little drawing of her spring quilt that she was already planning.

She went to sleep that night, completely content, a smile on her face.

CHAPTER NINE

With his mother and sister-in-law at the Lambright house, and Sawyer busy in the barn, Caleb couldn't let the opportunity to talk to his father pass him by. He needed advice—desperately so. It was finally time he told someone about his intent to court Abigail Fisher. Not to mention, he finally had *time* in the first place.

"Hey Pa, can I talk to you?" Caleb asked, approaching where his father sat by the fire.

"Always, my boy," he invited. Caleb took a seat in the companion rocker. "What do you need to talk about?"

"I want to court a girl," he confessed, barely managing to get the words out.

"That's wonderful news!" his father cheered with enthusiasm.

"But I'm too scared that the girl I like won't like how busy I am," Caleb admitted. "And she deserves to be given all the time in the world. But I can't, or won't rather, give up all of my work. I enjoy it too much. What should I do?"

His father nodded, silently pondering for a moment. Caleb turned to the fire, wanting to burn his cowardice away. Abigail wasn't like Collette in so many ways—but he could bear the thought of her breaking it off for the same reason.

"Who is it that has caught your eye?" his father asked.

"Abigail," he answered. He couldn't help but smile when he spoke her name. "Abigail Fisher."

"A fine lady," his father nodded. "From what your mother says, it seems as if they're two peas in a pod. Three if you count Bridget too."

"But after the new year begins, I won't have time to spend with her every day," Caleb sighed. "I have the time now, but that won't last forever."

"Well, then it wouldn't be as special if it happened every day," his father smiled. "Besides, have you ever thought that maybe Abigail wouldn't mind your time spend with work as much as Collette did?"

"Don't all women want to have time dedicated to them?" Caleb asked, confused.

His father laughed, "Of course they do. But some value the quality over quantity."

"Like Ma?" he asked.

"Just like Ma, and Bridget too," he smiled at Caleb. "That's how this whole quilting circle began, all those years ago. I was working on the farm, and your mother wanted some company as she was bedridden with Sawyer. So she invited a few friends over while I worked in the fields. That way, she was able to find connections with other people so that when she and I spend time together, it feels extra special."

"Abigail is always busy with something," Caleb admitted. "And I like that."

"So she'll respect you for your work as well," his father smiled brightly. "In fact, some of the best and strongest relationships come from people that keep themselves in a courtship. Yes, it's great to get lost in their eyes, but you have to stay in your mind and in your heart to love them completely. Two people can exist together as a couple without sacrificing so much of their identity."

"And what about her family? How do I ask?"

"Start with Mr. Lambright," his father laughed. "Ask him first. And if she really wants, you can write a letter to her family. That would be perfectly fine. In fact, that's what I did to court your mother."

"Really?"

"Oh yes, back when she was filling in as a teacher here," he smiled fondly. "I couldn't take the time to travel to Ohio for a proper asking, so I wrote her father. I waited until I got a response, but it was the longest three weeks of my life."

So Caleb sat and listened to his father talk of days in the early courtship with his mother. And when Sawyer came in from the barn, he joined them by the fire, listening as well. It had been a long time since the three

Graber men could sit and talk for any long period of time. And it felt nice.

Caleb smiled at all that he had, and time was bountiful to him, at least for tonight. He got to reconnect with Sawyer, who had been unnaturally busy lately because Bridget was expecting and the baby would be due in the early summer. He listened as his big brother, who always seemed to have everything figured out, asked their father for advice.

That night, when his mother and sister-in-law returned home, they sat around the fire and shared the story of their night. They were all one big family, and Caleb could just picture how well Abigail would fit in on nights like these.

Yes. Now was the perfect time.

CHAPTER TEN

Time seemed to move in a blur since the night the Grabers had visited. Suddenly, the holiday season was here, and children were singing Christmas hymns every night. Abigail felt that she was slowly running out of time to finish up her quilt for her sister and Aaron as a wedding present, along with smaller gifts for everyone else for the holidays.

It was a late snowy Saturday morning, two days before Christmas. She had wanted to go home for the holiday, but the roads were terribly covered with snow. And besides, she would be going soon enough for Trina and Aaron's wedding. She knew when that time came, the whole Lambright household would be going along with her to celebrate.

She realized she couldn't be happier for Aaron and her sister.

Most importantly, Abigail had hardly even thought about them at all. She had found that it hadn't bothered her anymore. Caleb was much more fascinating, and he was very supportive of her quilting. Not that Aaron or Trina weren't, but there was something in Caleb's compliments of her craft that had her heart soaring.

It was the day at the market when she found out the depth of his affections. After Caleb had sold his table, he had come to help his family sell the canned goods. They had gotten to talking, and he had confessed that he was the one that told Bishop Samuel of her Christmas quilt. She couldn't resist wrapping him in a grateful hug.

Since then, she had barely found time to sit down for an extended length of time. She was working on a new dress for Trina's wedding, along with all the gifts for her family. Abigail even enlisted Caleb's help in creating a small set of drawers for Aunt Eleanor and Patience, given how much scrap fabric the women had lying around at any given time.

But that Saturday morning had been all to herself. It was nice to sit by the fire and quilt with her aunt and cousin, quietly talking. The three of them continued to quilt away as the snow fell, making last-minute gifts for their extending family. It was a normal Saturday morning, the house smelling like fresh pie and pine. Abigail felt completely at home with where she was.

There was a knock at the door. The three of them paused their quilting. Abigail looked at Patience, who sat in the rocker and shrugged. But there was something off in her smile, as if she was hiding a secret. And the same smile was on Aunt Eleanor's face as well.

Uncle Wayne smiled cheerfully, going up to answer the door. The three women in the house stayed huddled by the fire. She heard mumbled voices and greetings, and two sets of feet returned to the living room. Soon, Caleb Graber was standing in front of them, looking bright and cheerful. He had his hat in his hand, and his hair was lightly dusted with snow and his cheeks pink from the breeze.

The scene looked too familiar to Abigail. But she had absolutely no doubt in

Caleb's affections for her. He had a large smile on his face, one so contagious that Abigail couldn't help but smile too. And based on the expression on Uncle Wayne's face, it had been a good conversation concerning their courtship.

"Mrs. Lambright, Miss Patience," he greeted. His eyes rested on her, and Abigail's heart soared higher than ever before. "Miss Abigail, would you like to join me for lunch?"

She smiled up at him and nodded. Somehow she knew that this was the timing God intended for them as a couple—when she had healed from her heartbreak and he and fulfilled his obligations. She stood up, wrapping her shawl around her as she said goodbye. Her family beamed with smiles, happy for both of them.

There was always enough time for love.

<u>ONE YEAR LATER</u>

Abigail walked into the home she shared with her husband. It was the day before Christmas Eve, and she had finally stitched the remaining pieces of her gift for Caleb. She simply couldn't wait for Christmas to give it to him; she had to do it tonight. Besides, she had other smaller gifts for her husband to give him on Christmas.

Their almost first year of marriage had been blissful, and their lives busy. But there was always time for each other, and Abigail never felt more loved than she did when she was with Caleb.

"Caleb, I'm home!" she called cheekily.

Her husband, always ready to greet her at the door, ran to her and took her in his arms. It was their ritual—whoever was home first always met the other at the door. Especially when they were busy with their separate lives, the time at the doorway always meant more than Abigail could imagine. And lately, it had been her coming home at sundown, always quilting with Aunt Eleanor and Patience to finish her gift in time.

She hid the wrapped present behind her back, smiling as she gave her husband a sweet kiss. Abigail had spent a good chunk of time at the Lambright house, trying to decide what wrapping paper would go best. She finally decided on the plain green paper, knowing that her husband would shred it anyways. He pulled away, his eyes lit with a smile, trying to sneak a peek at what she was hiding.

"What do you have there, love?" he asked with a grin.

"I have a present for you," she answered. "And I just can't wait until Christmas."

"I have a present for you too. It's in the living room," he smiled, rocking on his heels. "But you have to close your eyes."

Abigail set her quilting bag on the coat hooks that Caleb had made. Their house was a combination of their crafts in almost every aspect. The furniture was made mostly by Caleb, except for the Gospel study table for their breakfast nook that Uncle Wayne had made as a wedding present. And on their bed was the quilt that Abigail had made for her husband, the blanket containing scraps of fabric from her wedding dress and his suit.

Caleb gently placed his hands over her eyes, carefully leading her to the living room. Abigail held her present for Caleb, happy that he had something to give her in return. Even though neither of them had communicated their intentions, they just seemed to know that it was the right time to exchange. Abigail felt her husband lift his hands, but she kept her eyes closed.

"Okay, open your eyes," he said softly.

Abigail did and saw the most beautiful thing her husband had ever made. In the center of their living room was a quilt rack, stained a beautiful dark cherry color. Abigail had remembered how she mentioned that she liked the color in passing and turned to her husband. Caleb stood proud, and Abigail was almost in tears.

"You deserve to have such a beautiful display for your work, love," he smiled shyly. "And God gifted me so much extra time this year that I could make this for you. I know I haven't been home much, but I was just so excited for this."

"I love it, and I love you," she replied, tears of joy falling down her cheeks. She handed him the box she held. "I should also apologize that I haven't been home much either, though for the same reason."

Caleb looked at her quizzically before taking the box and, as expected, shredding the paper. Abigail laughed. Her husband's enthusiasm for the holidays, even as he grew older, never ceased to bring her joy as well. He opened the box, looked inside, and broke down in tears. Carefully, he set the box down on the floor, the quilt still inside, and wrapped Abigail in a hug.

"You're so incredibly talented," he whispered against her neck, the tears following his words. "And I am so extremely blessed that I am married to you. I love you, Abigail."

Abigail laughed, "You haven't even seen the whole thing."

With a renewed joy, Caleb broke his hug and went back to the box. Abigail knew what he had seen—the top panel was the stitched hay bales and crops of the Graber farm. Gently, Caleb lifted the rest of the quilt up, seeing the greens and golds of the farm swirl into the browns and tans of the woodshop, a rendition of his table displayed amongst the tools and wood-shaving design.

And in the middle was their little blue house, complete with its white trim and two little figures. The border was swirled with a delightful patchwork of Abigail's old dresses.

Caleb looked at her in awe. He wrapped the quilt around himself and then brought Abigail into the cocoon—it was big enough for the both of them, as planned. Abigail laughed as he peppered her face with brilliant small kisses before finally bringing his lips to her own.

Her husband carefully folded the quilt, and together they put it on the new quilt rack that would proudly stand right by their bookcase. Abigail turned to her husband, who brought her in his arms and held her. The couple stared at their gifts from each other in the glow of the firelight and smiled as Christmas hymns were sung by the kids down the street with such passion for the gift of Christ that you could hear them for miles.

After all, the best gifts were from the heart.

The End

Please Check out My Other Works

By checking out the link below

http://cleanromancepublishing.com/rbauth

Many thanks for taking the time to buy and read through this book.

It means lots to be supported by SPECIAL **readers like** YOU**.**

Hope you enjoyed the book; please support my writing by leaving an honest review to assist other readers.

.

With Regards,

Ruth Bawell